COFFEE WITH
Mozart

C O F F E E   W I T H

Mozart

JULIAN RUSHTON

FOREWORD BY SIR JOHN TAVENER

DUNCAN BAIRD PUBLISHERS

LONDON

Coffee with Mozart
Julian Rushton

Distributed in the USA and Canada by
Sterling Publishing Co., Inc.
387 Park Avenue South
New York, NY 10016-8810

This edition first published in the UK and USA in 2007 by
Duncan Baird Publishers Ltd
Sixth Floor, Castle House
75–76 Wells Street, London W1T 3QH

Managing Editors: Gill Paul and Peggy Vance
Co-ordinating Editors: Daphne Razazan and James Hodgson
Editor: Susannah Marriott
Assistant Editor: Kirty Topiwala
Managing Designer: Clare Thorpe

Library of Congress Cataloging-in-Publication Data Available
ISBN-10: 1-84483-513-8   ISBN-13: 978-1-84483-513-3
10 9 8 7 6 5 4 3 2 1
Printed in China

For information about custom editions, special sales, premium and corporate purchases, please contact Sterling Special Sales Department at 800-805-5489 or specialsales@sterlingpub.com.

Publisher's note:
The interviews in this book are purely fictional, while having a solid basis in biographical fact. They take place between a fictionalized Mozart and an imaginary interviewer.

CONTENTS

Foreword by SIR JOHN TAVENER

A lifelong love of Mozart began when I was 12 years old. My romantic and aristocratically beautiful godmother took me to see *The Magic Flute* at Glyndebourne. I was overwhelmed by the magic of this work and it has continued to overwhelm me with its beauty all through my life. It has only been recently, however, that I have tried to understand why I love Mozart beyond any other composer.

Mozart belongs to a historical age that does not attract me in the least—an age of superficiality and powdered hair. It seems unlikely that the most "sacred" composer of the West should emerge in that dilapidated era. Using the term "sacred" about Mozart may elicit some surprise, but I truly believe that Mozart's *Magic Flute* connects to Krishna's flute, just as his music in general can be compared to that particular kind of sacredness one finds in Persian and Hindu miniature paintings. I am not, of course, saying that Mozart himself was fully spiritually developed. God used this frail man to communicate to the world the eternal vision of childhood, and the divine world of Lila, a Sanskrit term meaning "divine play."

Mozart was faultlessly crystalline, and he was also the most natural composer that ever lived. His melodies, rhythms and harmonies seem as natural as virgin nature itself. Mozart's music, one might say, pre-existed. It required man to pluck it out from the spheres. His music is more feminine and more ecstatic than that of any composer I know. He makes the commonplace divine and everything he touches becomes sacred. He hears God everywhere and he sings His ecstasy in every single one of his operatic characters, from Sarastro to Papageno, to the Countess in *The Marriage of Figaro* and to Don Giovanni himself. He cannot help himself, for like the eternal child that he is, he never ceases to celebrate the ecstatic act of being.

Many pundits love to dwell on the Requiem or the doubtless remarkable entrance of the Commendatore in *Don Giovanni*, probably because these people love the innovatory. But paradoxically, for me, it is not in these moments that I perceive the divine in Mozart, but, for example, in Zerlina's unbearably beautiful "Vedrai Carino" in *Don Giovanni*. This invokes in me all the longing, and all the beauty and all the truth that I know: Zerlina by offering her beating heart to Masetto becomes the heartbeat of God seen through the eyes of a child. I so often play this music, and if you change one single note of it, it falls to pieces. The spacing of every simple and divine chord is so perfectly heard that once again it seems to belong to a celestial harmony.

Mozart is for me what the Sufis call a manifestation of the Essence of God. The fact that one can speak in such exalted terms about Mozart puts him in a unique category, and outside the whole canon of Western music. In his essence he has revealed paradise to me.

John Tavener

INTRODUCTION

Celebrations of the 250th anniversary of Mozart's birth have confirmed the composer's cultural prominence, matched among musicians only by J.S. Bach, Beethoven, and Wagner. Mozart is not the earliest composer still admired today, but no other has had so many works in the permanent core of the repertory for so long. Among his operas, *Figaro* is the yardstick for realistic comedy, *Don Giovanni* the inspiration of the Romantic movement, and *The Magic Flute* the foundation stone of German opera. Of his instrumental works, the concertos are central to the performance aspirations of violinists, wind players, and, above all, pianists. The quartets, quintets, and serenades are indispensable to the repertoire of smaller ensembles, while orchestras continually turn to the symphonies, especially the last two, in G minor and C major (the "Jupiter").

Mozart is a "classical" composer both in the broadest sense and also because he worked within the "classical" period (the late 18th and early 19th centuries). But "classical" does not imply coldness or austerity: Mozart's music bubbles with life. Comparison with his contemporaries, who used the same musical language, highlights Mozart's inventiveness in rhythm, melody, and harmony, and his skill in combining parts in counterpoint. His orchestral colors, too, are more varied and vivid.

Mozart did not have an easy life. He had to work hard and constantly at composition, but even his hackwork bears the stamp of his genius. His exceptional musical facility, evident from an unusually early age, emerged in performance, too. He was also a teacher and adviser to colleagues and fledgling musicians. His early brilliance made him the archetypal prodigy, or *Wunderkind*, and his relatively short lifespan makes his prolific output of great works all the more extraordinary. The circumstances of Mozart's death quickly became veiled by legend, some of the stories having a promotional value quickly recognized by his widow (whose later version of events is not always to be trusted).

The dialogues offered in this book are fiction, but not by any means implausible. Mozart was a friendly man, and, despite his egotism, a helpful one. Imagine, therefore, an English visitor to Vienna: a potential student, perhaps, or a scout for an opera or concert organization (Mozart received a number of invitations to visit London).

We find the composer in his last days, late in November 1791. He may already have contracted the infection that caused his death early in December.

Mozart had lost younger friends as well as his parents, and illness turns his thoughts toward his own death. His mind wanders now and then, and he has to be recalled to questions. Mozart's speech is like his letters—serious, but sometimes prone to whimsy and swift changes of mood and topic.

The dialogues review Mozart's life and achievements, his relationships with his social superiors and fellow artists, and his religious and political beliefs. Leitmotifs include his extraordinary upbringing, Mozart's reception in his lifetime, his precarious finances, and his most intense relationship—with his remarkable father, Leopold. But it is Mozart's musicality that hijacks the conversations, as he remembers a flood of wonderful compositions.

WOLFGANG AMADEUS MOZART
(1756–1791)
His Life in Short

The name "Mozart" triggers certain ideas—a composer of beautiful music that's a pleasure to listen to; a *Wunderkind* (wonder child) and genius; a neglected artist who died young and was buried as a pauper. The first two impressions are correct, but the last one does not withstand examination. Mozart died aged 35, having been a mature artist since his teens. His obituaries place him among the most famous musicians in Europe—he accomplished an immense body of work, and was among the greatest virtuosi of his age. He died of natural causes, and was decently, if inexpensively, buried. It is true that he was in debt, but death came when his prospects were improving—and, ironically, while he was working on a Mass for the dead. Such romantic circumstances naturally gave rise to myth-making.

Mozart's father, Leopold (1719–87), was an excellent violinist and able composer, and he rose to the rank of vice-*Kapellmeister* (Musical Director) at the court of the Prince-Archbishop of Salzburg.

Maria Anna Mozart, née Pertl (1720–78), bore her husband seven children. Only two survived infancy: Maria Anna Walburga Ignatia (familiarly Nannerl), born in July 1751, and Joannes Chrysostomus Wolfgangus Theophilus, born on January 27, 1756. The boy's first two names were rarely used. In the family he was Wolfgang, familiarly Woferl. Outside the family, he was Mozart—even to his wife. Rather than Theophilus ("beloved of God" in ancient Greek), the family used the German equivalent, Gottlieb; the Latin version of the phrase, Amadeus, became standard only after his death.

Mozart's life divides broadly into two. Up to 1780, the small independent state of Salzburg was his home, the center he traveled to and from. His last decade was spent in Vienna, capital of the Habsburg Empire. Anecdotal evidence suggests that by his fifth year, Mozart was playing the keyboard and trying to compose. He became competent on the violin, and later played its larger cousin, the viola, in chamber music, but he was first renowned as a keyboard prodigy. On his travels, Mozart assimilated foreign languages and styles of music as naturally as breathing. He never attended school, but his education was not exclusively musical. He was interested in mathematics, read widely, and became aware of the intellectual currents of the day.

Leopold soon realized that his gifted children (Nannerl, too, was a talented musician) offered him a chance to escape from Salzburg. The city was isolated and perceived—particularly by Wolfgang in later life—as provincial, but its nobility and clerics were well connected elsewhere in the Empire, and their relations were often helpful patrons. The family's first sorties to Munich and Vienna (1762) initiated contact with the Habsburg monarchy itself—a relationship fraught with difficulty, though often beneficial. Beginning in June 1763, the family's next tour lasted more than three years and was documented in lengthy bulletins intended for circulation in Salzburg, to maintain Leopold's standing there.

In Germany, Paris, and London, the child Mozart met leading musicians and played before select audiences, aristocratic and intellectual. The musical culture of London, where the family lived for over a year, was predominantly Italian, which suited the Mozarts (who despised French music). The city had also attracted German musicians, notably Handel, dead but not forgotten, and Johann Christian Bach, youngest son of Johann Sebastian. In London, Mozart composed keyboard music, and his first sonatas were published. He also took singing lessons. The children were objects of curiosity and quasi-scientific investigation: a report on them was presented to the Royal Society.

On their return journey, the family visited Holland and revisited Paris, before arriving back in Salzburg in November 1766. Leopold had received praise and money—as well as gifts such as snuffboxes, which he may have used as currency once home. Did his modest profits justify exposing his children to the rigors of travel? Perhaps not. But Leopold sincerely believed that God had entrusted him with a miracle that must be shown to the world.

Leopold continued his project of escape from Salzburg, hoping that he would eventually earn a well-paid position as a *Kapellmeister* on the back of his son's gifts. Mozart, who was all the time increasing in musical maturity, was soon competing on equal terms with his elders, producing part of an oratorio (*Die Schuldigkeit des ersten Gebotes*, "The Obligation of the First Law"), a short Latin opera (*Apollo et Hyacinthus*), and prodigious amounts of sacred music. Opportunities for secular music included serenades to celebrate the end of the university's academic year, combining elements of the symphony and concerto. Mozart also wrote concertos for local or visiting musicians, including five for violin and his first keyboard concertos, and several symphonies.

He longed to compose operas, and these were his main chance for success abroad. In 1767–68 a visit to Vienna was disrupted by a smallpox epidemic, and the Mozarts fled to Bohemia. Back in Vienna,

Emperor Joseph II's keen interest in the theater led Leopold to believe he had ordered an opera from his young genius. The theater management thought otherwise, and questioned the boy's capability. Mozart's first *opera buffa* (Italian comedy), *La finta semplice*, was rejected. Leopold's subsequent fury may have alienated the Italian musicians in Vienna, whom he distrusted (in Vienna as in Salzburg, they were routinely paid more than Germans of equivalent skill). More seriously, Leopold may have annoyed the imperial family. Before the Mozarts went home, honor was partially restored by performances of the 12-year old's first German opera, the short comedy *Bastien und Bastienne* (1768), and his first large-scale setting of the Catholic Mass.

Mozart's first visit to Italy lasted more than a year (1769–71), and took in Rome (where at 14 he was knighted by the Pope) and Naples. His father accompanied him; his mother and sister remained at home—the first division of the family group. In Milan, the friendly Austrian governor commissioned the boy to write an *opera seria* (a serious opera in Italian), and *Mitridate* was successfully performed on December 26, 1770. Two commissions followed from Milan, requiring separate journeys. Archduke Ferdinand, taking over the reins of government, commissioned a short opera for his marriage, *Ascanio in Alba* (1771). Leopold Mozart, with more glee than tact, reported that the piece outshone the full-scale serious opera by the distinguished and elderly Saxon composer Hasse, a favorite of the Archduke's mother, Empress Maria Theresia. The second commission, and the more successful, was another *opera seria*, *Lucio Silla*, performed two years to the day after *Mitridate*. Mozart never returned to Italy.

Meanwhile drastic change came to Salzburg with the death in 1771 of the ruling Prince-Archbishop Schrattenbach, who had allowed, even encouraged, the Mozarts to travel without jeopardizing Leopold's employment in the Salzburg court. Schrattenbach's successor, Hieronymus Colloredo, took a dim view of such activities, and so he becomes the principal villain of the Mozart story. The boy was now paid for his work as violinist and composer in the cathedral, but Colloredo discouraged elaborate sacred music. Mozart had composed a sententious operatic allegory (*Il sogno di Scipione*, "Scipio's Dream") to celebrate Schrattenbach's 50th year in the priesthood. It was adjusted to inaugurate Colloredo's reign, but his next opportunity to write an opera at home came only in 1775 (*Il re pastore*). Just before this, he was allowed to present a new *opera buffa* (*La finta giardiniera*) in Munich. In 1777, Mozart sought leave to travel with his father; it was denied, and Leopold nearly lost his job. Mozart was summarily dismissed. Now aged almost 22, he set out with his mother to seek a position in Germany or his fortune in Paris.

Away from his father, Mozart tasted independence and responsibility. He was also free to consider personal relationships. In Augsburg in Bavaria (Leopold's birthplace), he became close to a cousin, Maria Anna Thekla, to whom he directed a few mildly improper letters (often misread as evidence that he was habitually foul-mouthed). Reluctant to leave Germany, he spent the winter of 1777–78 in Mannheim, home to Europe's most brilliant orchestra under the lavish patronage of the Elector Palatine, Carl Theodor. Mozart became firm friends with the musicians, but tactlessly alienated the vice-*Kapellmeister*, Abbé Vogler, by making too obvious his low opinion of the older man's abilities. In Mannheim, Mozart composed his first mature sonatas, and wrote quartets and concertos for Ferdinand Dejean, an amateur flautist. Mozart took students, and was bewitched by a promising young singer, Aloysia Weber. Leopold ordered his son on to Paris, but there he made little headway against vested interests in the operatic and concert worlds, though a new symphony (the "Paris") was successfully performed. But disaster struck: Mozart's mother fell ill and died in July 1778. Mozart declined an organist's post in Versailles, which lies about 10 miles from Paris. Instead of returning immediately to Salzburg, he dithered in Mannheim, although Carl Theodor, now Elector of Bavaria, had gone to Munich with his entourage, including Aloysia. Mozart moved on there, but Aloysia received him coldly. Heartbroken, he dragged himself home in January 1779.

The composer returned to familiar routines, creating outstanding church music: the "Coronation" Mass (1779) and the magnificent "Vesperae solennes de confessore" (1780). Nevertheless, Colloredo regarded him with disfavor. Perhaps Mozart devoted too much energy to work outside the terms of his employment: from this period come further excellent symphonies (numbers 32–34 in the conventional ordering), the superb *Sinfonia concertante* for violin and viola, and theater music, including most of an opera (*Zaide*) that he probably hoped would interest the newly formed German opera company (National-Singspiel) in Vienna, or the touring company that was giving *La finta giardiniera* in German.

In 1780 came another commission from Munich. Colloredo granted Mozart leave to compose and direct *Idomeneo*, a mythological opera of profound seriousness and moral weight. Although it was well received, no appointment followed, and Mozart was forced to obey a summons to Vienna, where Colloredo was spending the winter. Mozart quickly decided that he must stay in the city, even though he knew this would cost him his job. For Leopold it was a disaster; for Wolfgang, freedom. Through talent and hard work, he established himself in Vienna, happily sacrificing a regular salary in exchange for independence. He took pupils; he published chamber and keyboard music for single payments (there were no royalties on sales); he played in public, in private houses, and at court. Mozart was soon commissioned by the German opera company. *Die Entführung aus dem Serail* (literally "The Abduction from the Harem," known as *The Seraglio*) received a triumphant première in 1782. For operas, he received a flat fee, with no payment for later performances or productions. Today, this opera, which was soon performed all over Germany, would have provided him with a useful income.

Then the Emperor bowed to public taste for opera in Italian, and replaced the German opera company with an Italian *buffo* troupe. This was a setback for Mozart: for four years he wrote no operas. But he did well with subscription concerts, for which he wrote the first supreme masterpieces of the piano concerto. And he continued to study, notably older music (Bach and Handel), to which he was introduced by an important patron, Baron van Swieten. As an unforeseen consequence, Mozart complicated and enriched his musical language, sometimes beyond what the market seems to have wanted. This made composition more difficult for him, and his music harder for amateurs. But real musicians appreciated him—in 1785 Joseph Haydn told Leopold that his son was "the greatest composer I know."

In 1782, to Leopold's opposition, Mozart married Constanze Weber, a less distinguished singer than her elder sisters Aloysia and Josepha. She became a loyal and affectionate partner and bore Mozart six children, of whom four died in infancy. The couple visited Salzburg once, in 1783. Nannerl, whose chances of a musical career had been sacrificed to her brother, married a widower with several children. She disapproved of Constanze, probably less on personal grounds than because the family unit was disrupted. Nannerl became estranged from her brother and is partly responsible for the legend that Constanze was frivolous and an incapable housekeeper.

Mozart's solid position in Viennese society by the mid-1780s is attested to by "the very fine apartment with all the furniture he needs" witnessed by Leopold on a visit in 1785. The respectability is confirmed by his status as a Freemason. But Mozart's concert-giving suffered a decline, his teaching was not lucrative (he may sometimes have taken no fees), sales of his music brought in little, and in 1787 the family moved to cheaper lodgings. An alternative source of revenue appeared as Mozart re-entered the arena of Italian opera. Here, his formidable rivals included the Spanish composer Vicente Martín y Soler (known as Martini), resident Italians including the court composer Antonio Salieri, and Italians such as Giovanni Paisiello who visited or whose works were imported into Vienna. Salieri has been unjustly maligned as a jealous rival of Mozart. It seems clear that they were not friends, but, if anyone was jealous, it was Mozart, for Salieri was well established, successful, and well paid. Of these composers, the most popular were Paisiello and Martín. The new court poet Lorenzo Da Ponte wrote opera texts (librettos) for Martín and Salieri, but in 1785 agreed to work for Mozart on a sequel to Paisiello's opera *Il barbiere di Siviglia* ("The Barber of Seville").

The resulting opera, *Le nozze di Figaro* ("The Marriage of Figaro"), was given at the court theater in May 1786. It was a *succès d'estime*, although performances were interrupted by the departure of the leading singer, Nancy Storace, and the triumph of Martín's *Una cosa rara* at the same theater. It is suggested that the portrayal of a licentious aristocrat in *Figaro* caused offense, but this is unlikely: a similar character featured prominently in Martín's opera, and *Figaro* was successfully revived in August 1789. Later in 1786, the Bohemian capital, Prague, was smitten by Figaromania. There, Mozart produced a fine symphony, the "Prague" (1787), and received a new opera commission. Back in Vienna, he composed two great string quintets, and worked on the opera *Don Giovanni*. In May 1787, Leopold

Mozart, still somewhat embittered by his son's desertion of the family project, died in Salzburg. *Don Giovanni* was triumphantly produced in Prague that autumn, but met with less success in Vienna the following May; there followed several productions elsewhere, in German, under the title *Don Juan*.

In the summer of 1788, Mozart should have been at the height of his prosperity. He was incredibly productive in this period, writing his three last symphonies and a group of piano trios. Yet begging letters survive, addressed to a brother Freemason, Michael Puchberg. What had gone wrong? Wealthy Viennese may have had less to spend on culture because of Emperor Joseph's decision to make war on the Ottoman Empire in 1788. But any decline in Mozart's income from teaching and concert-giving should have been offset by opera fees and the salary Joseph awarded him as *Kammermusikus* (Imperial

Chamber Musician). We have few hard figures attesting to Mozart's income; he probably spent it rather than saving. The occasional luxury (a carriage, a billiard table) could be re-sold, but the costs of decent clothes, rent, and doctors' fees were unavoidable. Both Wolfgang and Constanze suffered periods of ill-health, and she was sent to the spa at Baden, near Vienna. At his death Mozart was in debt, but had good prospects. We may compare him to a modern family man who, not expecting to die yet, owes money for goods bought with credit cards.

In 1789 Mozart visited northern Germany (the musical King of Prussia in his sights), but gained little more than a substantial debt to his traveling companion, Count Lichnowsky. In January 1790, Da Ponte and Mozart produced their third opera, *Così fan tutte*. Performances were interrupted by the death of the Emperor. Mozart traveled to Frankfurt-am-

Main for the coronation of Joseph's brother Leopold II as Holy Roman Emperor. Leopold retained Mozart as *Kammermusikus*, but dismissed Da Ponte, and Mozart wrote nothing more for the court theater.

In 1791, after two years of lower productivity (which nevertheless included masterly chamber music), Mozart composed freely across several genres. He also wrote two new operas. *Die Zauberflöte* ("The Magic Flute"), a miraculous blend of rough comedy and spirituality, was composed for Emanuel Schikaneder's suburban Viennese Theater auf der Wieden. *La clemenza di Tito* was commissioned by the Prague nobility to celebrate Leopold's coronation as King of Bohemia. This was well received, and *The Magic Flute* was a triumph. Mozart also worked, unpaid, at St. Stephen's Cathedral in Vienna (he was promised the organist's post when the elderly incumbent died). He received a commission for a requiem Mass, but had first to finish a clarinet concerto and a cantata for the Freemasons.

In mid-November 1791, Mozart contracted an infection. The panacea of the time, bloodletting, proved useless, and the disease attacked his vital organs. When the doctor tried to reduce his fever with ice, Mozart lost consciousness and died a few hours later, on December 5. Devastated, Constanze pulled herself together with the help of friends. She secured a pension for herself, arranged performances and publication of Mozart's music, and, with second husband Georg Nikolaus Nissen, wrote a biography of the composer. The Mozarts' elder son Carl Thomas (1784–1858) became a government official; the younger, Franz Xaver (1791–1844), was a competent musician who, perhaps unwisely, styled himself W.A. Mozart junior. Neither son married, and neither, so far as is known, fathered any children.

NOW LET'S START TALKING …

Over the following pages, Mozart engages in an imaginary conversation covering fifteen themes, responding freely to searching questions.

The questions are in green italic type; Mozart's answers are in black type.

MOZART THE MAN

Perceptions of Mozart vary from the saintly
to the giggling idiot of Milos Forman's film
Amadeus, based on Peter Shaffer's play of the
same name. The truth is less outlandish. Mozart
was obsessed with music. In these conversations
his mind turns to music even if this interrupts a
train of thought, and he defines himself mainly
in relation to other musicians. His high self-
evaluation is evident, but this did not prevent
Mozart from being gregarious, and he was a loyal
friend who lent as well as borrowed money.

*Herr Mozart! Please excuse me for accosting you. You
don't know me, but we have acquaintances in London:
Signora Storace and her brother, and Mr. Kelly. May I
explain myself? I'm a keen lover of music, and I'm eager
to know more of the greatest musician living in Vienna.*

Sir, you flatter me. And I must confess, although I'm
happy to meet you, today I don't feel well . .

*I'm so sorry. May I offer you something in this hostelry?
Some coffee, maybe? If you have time, we could talk
quietly? I'd be most grateful.*

Yes, very well. Perhaps I shall feel better for a little
food, and perhaps for now a glass of beer.

(After sitting down and ordering) *Herr Mozart, your
color's returned! May I ask you a few questions about*

yourself? Perhaps you could start by describing yourself.

That's hard. I've been many things to many people.
A child prodigy—*Wunderkind*—on display at court.
I loved those pretty clothes! I've been a jobbing
musician, turning out Masses, serenades, operas
to commission. Concertos and arias for friends—
everything for an occasion. I'm a producer of
music. Whatever you need, I'll write it. Like a court
poet—or a cow giving milk! That still goes on. Those
recent pieces for a wretched mechanical organ—all
creaking and squeaking—for a waxwork show. But
they're good pieces. Most composers would have
turned out trash and taken the money. In Vienna
some "commissions" were my own, like the piano
concertos for my own concerts. But there are always
other jobs—if my sister-in-law Aloysia needs an
aria, I write one. Stadler needs a clarinet concerto:

I deliver. I got the court job: *Kammermusikus*,
Imperial Chamber Musician. Not *Kapellmeister*, oh
no, not the top job. Though I don't mind people
calling me *Kapellmeister*! It was my father's dream
that I'd become a famous *Kapellmeister*. And now
I'm a church musician again, at St. Stephen's …

*All this describes you professionally. Do you mind if
I return to you, to yourself? What kind of man are you?*

I'm a simple man. Honest in my dealings. I pay my way.

Excuse me, but it's rumored that you're in debt.

Is it? Well, rumor is sometimes true … Oh, yes, I'm
often in debt. Who isn't, in Vienna? I have to keep
up my position—I can't *not* spend money on clothes.
Yes, I *still* like good clothes, and if I didn't dress well,

who'd let me into their houses to teach and play? I got rid of the coach. I thought having one would save money, but no. One learns! Alas, the billiard table ... that had to go, too. My debts will be paid ... somehow. I'm not good with money, but I'm honest—in all ways. I don't cheat on my wife. Three years ago I thought my poor Constanze would die, she was so ill. Those doctors do their best to bankrupt a fellow. Now my son's at a decent school—that's not free, either.

Forgive me, but isn't it a little vain to spend so much on your appearance?

All right. For this nice beer, I forgive you! Yes, I *do* like my hair properly set and powdered, but that's necessary when I go to court, or to teach—and before the barber comes I've been up for hours, composing. I am *not* lazy! Papa said I didn't practice the violin properly, but I had to compose, and practice the clavier. One can't do everything. Perhaps I'm selfish and too absorbed in work, but it's produce or starve. But when I leave off working, I feel free, unbuttoned. I make silly jokes. Surely among friends nobody minds a few canons [rounds] with rude words. We all need to relax—and they're good canons …

But you're still telling me about music, about work.

Touché. But I enjoy games, and a walk in the park, and sleep—and, you know, when Constanze is at home … we enjoy … you understand … we've had six children, you know! Only two are living …

I'm sorry. Some coffee now, or another beer?

Thank you. I will—the beer, if you'd be so kind.

MOZART AND HIS PEERS

Mozart's music was often considered difficult—more the product of art (artificiality) than of the spontaneity and naturalness considered essential in an age influenced by the philosopher Jean-Jacques Rousseau. Nevertheless, his reputation stood high at the time of this conversation, in 1791. As for his views of others, Mozart inherited a paranoid streak from his father with respect to Italian musicians, but would also give credit where due. Among them were the traveling virtuoso and composer Muzio Clementi, whom Emperor Joseph set against him in a "contest," and the court composer long established in Vienna, Antonio Salieri.

How do you appear to other musicians? Are you convinced you're better than they are?

Yes. I'll be frank, I'm sure I'm better. Papa thought I was a gift from God. I don't know about that, but I started young, I worked hard, I learned from the best models from all over Europe. In the end it comes down to this: who else could write *Don Giovanni*, my clavier concertos, or my Symphony in C Major?

Surely you've written more than one in that key?

Of course. I mean the one I wrote, how long, three years ago—yes, just after my daughter died—at the same time I composed the one in G minor that Salieri conducted last spring. I added clarinets for that— wonderful, the sound of an orchestra with flutes, oboes, *and* clarinets ... Not even Papa Haydn—and

I revere him absolutely—not even he has written such symphonies.

Don't other composers resent such superiority?

Some … and not only Italians. The best understand. Paisiello compliments me—and his operas are played more than mine. So are Martini's (a bit of an ass, but a good fellow). Then Clementi!—all brilliance, all right hand—no taste, no heart. I called him "charlatan"—not to his face, just to my sister. He praised my playing, and I think he meant it. My left-hand work, you know, was something new. Now the young people—Hummel, Beethoven—will outstrip me, but that's how it goes! I was too harsh with Clementi, for he does have talent.

But in Paris, that fellow Cambini didn't appreciate me. Perhaps I shouldn't have played him his own

music with improvements … but I can't help myself.
I see how it could go better!

Most of the German composers were friendly.
Though not that bungler Vogler in Mannheim. When
I was young, the London Bach was kind. I admired
him greatly. Also Hasse. And Myslivecek, poor
fellow. Mamma said I shouldn't see him in Munich.
His face was eaten away—some disease he caught
from loose women. I hope he enjoyed it at the time,
poor fellow. I've never risked my health that way!

Then there's all my friends in Mannheim—that
orchestra! And now in Vienna there's Stadler. What
a player, what an inventor! His extended clarinet
is beautiful—those extra low notes, so hollow, so
sweet. He's just played my new concerto in Prague.
Leutgeb—a cheesemonger, and so a useful friend—
I'm writing him a new horn concerto—my fourth! He
runs out of breath nowadays, and can't hit the high

notes. Each concerto has to be easier than the one before! But such tone, such skill with his hands.

Tell me about your relationship with Salieri. Are you jealous of him?

Not really. He's not a bad old thing. Not much older than me—he just seems so. And, yes, not a bad composer. I was too friendly with "his" librettist—yes, Da Ponte. He blamed Da Ponte when their first opera failed. But then Salieri saw what Da Ponte could do with Martini and me! Then Salieri began the *School for Lovers* but gave up. He wasn't pleased when I made a success of it! But he respects my music—he used it for the Coronation of our new Emperor—and he liked *The Magic Flute* as well. Of course, he didn't want to write *German* opera, so he was quite happy to sit in my box and call it a Grand Opera, *operone*.

Singers, like Cavalieri, are my friends, too. I get on well with them—they know I understand their needs. Schikaneder's singers, Schack and Gerl, compose quite well—*The Philosopher's Stone* last year, they wrote some of that, and the *Anton* opera. I made clavier variations on one of their tunes. Singers, yes. Storace was the best actress. Sang quite well, too. That Irish chap, O'Kelly, I liked. You know him I gave him a few tips on composing—waste of breath … Earlier than that there was Adamberger (Belmonte in *The Seraglio*), a brother Mason and a good friend.

What about Madame Lange?

Ah, Aloysia … my sister-in-law. It's an open secret that I was in love with her! Constanze knew all about that, of course—we were together in Mannheim, but it was over before the Webers moved to Vienna. Aloysia, yes, we were cold to one another for a while, but we're over that. Her husband is painting my portrait. It's not finished, but we like it so far! He did my father, too—just a sketch, I don't know what's become of it. To these people I appear as I am. I am one of them.

But better?

Yes, if you insist. I think I'm better. As a pianist and composer, not a singer! And not a painter … But now I'm older, people respect my achievements. And I help them—I play in their concerts. They sing for me, I play for them. When Storace left Vienna, I wrote that aria with piano obbligato for her farewell concert— that was special! Also, I have students. Keep your eye on that little boy, Hummel. He lived with us for a year. No fee, but it's worth it to watch such a talent grow.

AN ORDINARY HUSBAND

None of the posthumous rumors that Mozart
was promiscuous and unfaithful to his wife
Constanze has been substantiated. Singers—
Cavalieri, Storace, Duschek—have been linked
romantically with Mozart without evidence.
Clearly he loved a good soprano voice, and was
ready to joke with women as well as write for
them. But there is no reason to assume that
Mozart was hypocritical about sexual matters,
nor that his premature death was the result of
loose living.

What of the women in your life?

Surely you don't expect me to confess to a stranger!
No, seriously. Before Constanze, there was Aloysia.
And before that, I was a bit in love with my cousin
because we liked the same silly jokes. Since you
ask—no need to say it, I can see it in your face—we
liked to make merry talking about what comes out
from behind! Papa and Mamma were fond of such
jokes, too. So were those jolly people in Mannheim—
Wendling the flute-player, Cannabich for all that he
was *Kapellmeister*. A good drink, a few rude jokes,
singing, and no harm done. Happy days! But my
cousin, she's not married, and had a child—that's
bad. Maybe I could have saved her …

*Please—surely that's not your fault. But tell me more
about your singers.*

[50]

Mine, are they, now? Oh, so many! A few bitches, but more real friends. Duschek, she's a one. Locked me in the summerhouse until I'd written her an aria. That was in Prague, the *Don Giovanni* time. I tried to avenge myself. I made it awkward—you know, tricky intervals—but she could sing anything at sight. She's a rare friend. Sings my music even if I'm not around—most people don't do that. Some singers made me change things, but then the arias have to suit the singer. I'm a musical milliner! I fit the costume to the figure. Then it's a success for her, and a success for me.

Are women singers harder to please than men?

No. The worst was that tenor in Milan. What was the name, Ettore? He insisted on singing some Italian's aria, in *my* opera. No one else did that to me. Of course, I've written pieces for other people's operas, but they weren't around to get annoyed! And I always did it to make a better impression. There was an opera from Italy not written for our singers, and it didn't suit Aloysia. Such a special voice, those pure high notes. I did the same improvement jobs for my own operas—new arias for Ferrarese in *Figaro* (she was Da Ponte's *inamorata*, you know, I had to oblige those two!). But I prefer the original arias that I wrote for Storace … Did you hear they've both been dismissed now—Ferrarese and Da Ponte?

Yes, indeed. Weren't you just a little in love with your singers?

Not in *that* way! I'm not like Da Ponte's friend Casanova. Just an ordinary husband … and a working man.

THE COMPOSER AT WORK

Legends about Mozart's composing methods—some based on a posthumously forged letter—suggest that he had superhuman powers of concentration and memory. The historical evidence indicates that he worked in a regular way, at the keyboard or on paper. Moreover, although his manuscripts are clear and confidently written, he did sometimes make mistakes. Several of Mozart's unfinished works were completed after his death by others (undetected for years); many more have been completed recently.

You're the finest pianist in Germany. Why did you compose so much?

Your question puzzles me: musicians compose. Of course, I played other composers' music—mostly when I was too young to have written anything better! And I compose for money.

Isn't there more money in performing?

Sometimes. But 100 ducats for an opera—that's not bad! And now 50 ducats for a requiem—easy!

Easy? If you say so. But tell me, how do you compose?

How? Why? What funny questions! I *like* to compose above everything, even playing. Though that's often much the same …

How so? Do you need a clavier to compose?

Of course not! What a question ... Ah, the beer's coming. Please excuse me, I'm still thirsty ... (*To the waiter*) Thank you.

I shall try to answer straightforwardly. I prefer having a clavier handy. But the clavier's not for inventing things, it's for linking them by improvising. Yes, stringing ideas together. You know how we like contrast—*chiaroscuro*—in modern music? Different ideas in the same tempo, shifting colors, light and dark, major and minor harmony. Enchanting! And it keeps the listener interested. I learned that from the London Bach, a dear man and a great composer. It was sad he died so young—though older than I am now ... What were we talking about?

Stringing ideas together.

Yes. Papa called it "*il filo*," the thread that binds ideas together. But he was worried that I made things too difficult. I remember that letter well—I think I was in Mannheim: "Small things are great if done in a natural way—if they flow smoothly and are well composed. It's harder to do that than write artificial harmonies that most people don't understand …" Maybe it was "harder" for him, it wasn't for me. What else did he say? "Good composition and arrangement of ideas, *il filo*—thus you can tell the maestro from the clodhopper, even in trivial works …" Of course, this was all about selling printed music. Or making flute quartets for that Dutch doctor in Mannheim. What was his name—Deschamps? Dejean? Papa was angry when I only completed half the commission …

Improvising in public's different. Then you can play things that messieurs-les-amateurs delight in, but wouldn't like written down. Bold dissonances,

like in old Bach's works. Lines that clash, but
logically, so they separate and work into a more
beautiful consonance. Fugues. So hard to write!

But you played them on the spur of the moment?

Yes, of course. Then you get away with things—change
key quickly, bring in the main idea—and everyone
calls "Bravo!" But getting everything in place on paper,
so it's bearable to repeat, that's another thing. And
not just with fugues. The contrast—the *chiaroscuro*—
needs great care. You have to introduce surprises,
but in a way that will please, that connoisseurs
understand and amateurs like, too … though they
won't know why. And if you're not careful, the thread
will break!

Does your thread never break?

Maybe … it did when I was young. But I'm usually happy with what I've done. I can take or leave my older works. Those with long ears will leave the new ones, too. It's their problem, if they've paid for them! Some rich oaf bought my quartets, the ones I dedicated to Papa Haydn and that cost me so much time and were so difficult to write. Not paid back in sales, I can tell you! But this ass, he starts to play them with his lackeys, and stops and says the music is full of mistakes—and he throws it away! But they were well printed. No mistakes.

Perhaps the music was difficult …

Not the finger-work, it's the notes themselves. But they all make sense—go over them, *practice*, until you can hear the harmony. It's not meant to be easy. Whatever Papa said, connoisseurs have rights as well!

FROM PUPIL TO TEACHER

Mozart studied music from direct experience—
by playing and listening. Ensemble music
was usually published in separate parts, for
performance, rather than aligned in a score,
for study. Mozart is said to have laid out the
eight separate parts of a Bach motet on the
floor, fitting the music together in his head.
His patron, Baron van Swieten, the Imperial
librarian and censor, had a fine collection of
manuscripts for study, and preferred older,
or dead, composers, unusually for an era that
valued novelty. Mozart was a strict teacher,
following the techniques of traditional
counterpoint codified in J.J. Fux's book *Gradus
ad Parnassum* (1725).

Who were your teachers?

Papa, of course. "After God comes Papa ..." As a child
I used to say that. But even he couldn't do everything.
Keyboard (I learned so much from Nannerl), violin,
composition—these I learned from Papa and other
Salzburg musicians (some weren't so bad). Then in
London there was the English Bach. But mostly I
learned by listening, watching, and talking! Bach
didn't give real lessons, and I was only eight. I learned
singing from Manzuoli, the castrato. I was happy he
came to sing my *Ascanio* later, in Milan. But the old
fool refused his fee because it wasn't enough!

    Mostly I learn from music, not from people.
By playing chamber music and in the orchestra.
And from operas—even by old Hasse and Gluck. I
can hear what fits the singers, what works in the
orchestra and theater. And what doesn't! Gluck?

Sometimes beautiful, sometimes crude. I learned
from composers I didn't even meet. If I met them
later I could play their music to them … with
improvements, if I wasn't careful!

You would play from memory?

I have a good memory! But I can also read music. I
lay the parts out on the floor—violin one, violin two,
viola, cello—then piece them together in my head.
That's the way to learn. Papa Haydn's quartets, for
instance. I can learn from dead people by hearing
their music, reading their music.

It's said that you transcribed Allegri's Miserere *because
it wasn't allowed out of the Sistine chapel.*

Yes. But it's a very simple piece. It taught me nothing!

So what dead composers did you learn from?

Most of all Handel and old Bach, from those Sunday afternoons at Swieten's—strange pompous man, thought music was going to the dogs. He preferred the older Bach brothers, not my London friend. At first I thought this ancient music was just a bit of fun and I was ready to sneer, but the music took me over. I learned so much—from Bach most of all. Now, *there* was a musician—him I bow to—I don't think I'm better than *him*! You can hear all this in my best music. Not just the fugues—everywhere, if you have ears.

Do you pass on these lessons to your own students?

Some can learn, some never will … There are young ladies who do music to help find a husband. They give up when they marry (just as well, perhaps). That girl in Paris, daughter of that flute-playing duke—Duc de Guines. She played the harp well, but compose? She wanted me to write her music for her. And I had to complain before I was paid.

And your composition students? How do you teach them?

Composition and playing go together. Little Hummel, he has what I had as a child—mimicry and a good memory. He should do well. That English lad—Thomas Attwood—he might do all right. He'd been to Italy, but still I had to teach him basics. Perhaps you know him? Yes, it was good to talk English a little. But I'm glad your German is so good. I'm not sure I could carry on a conversation in English, even if I were feeling better … Yes, Attwood. He made bad mistakes sometimes, so I wrote in his book, "You are an ass." Ask him to show you … No, perhaps not. But he went home just as he was getting somewhere. It's often so. Hummel was taken off by his father to tour. A new *Wunderkind*, a second Mozart, they call him. I can hardly complain about that!

Do you enjoy teaching composition?

It's better than teaching piano to the rich and untalented, or even to that ugly Auernhammer girl, who plays very well. Babette Ployer—a better pianist than composer—she played my concertos. Freystädtler was all right, but dull. Süssmayr, a useful fellow. Helpful. But anything good of his is copied from me. My methods? The usual: Fux's *Steps to Parnassus*. Counterpoint, as I learned from Padre Martini in Bologna—a dear, good man, a musical saint. Harmony in four parts, then short pieces—minuets—with proper harmony, and the basses making good counterpoint. That kind of thing. Invention comes or it doesn't, but it's no use without technique. You begin something. If the ideas seem good, technique comes in to extend them, to finish the texture. But maybe another piece is more urgent, so you have to put what you were working on to one side.

Do you always finish your pieces, eventually?

I'm afraid not. I have many unfinished beginnings in my desk. You might wonder how I've managed to complete so many! I don't compose just for my own satisfaction. I compose because it's my life—my inner life—but also because my family must eat …

I understand that, but why would you not complete something?

No sale! Fugues? I *could* have finished them. I
did finish them when I played them! I sent one to
Nannerl—don't play it too fast, I said. As if one could,
with that crunching counterpoint. The Emperor—
Joseph, that is—liked them, but who else?

Sonatas? Quintets? Variations? Sometimes I
can sell a few sonatas, so I pick them up and finish
them, and there's a few gulden to pay the doctor.
Even concertos I can profit from—by playing them
in my concerts. My newest clavier concerto I began
two years ago, and finished in time for Beer's benefit
concert last January. Earlier there was no chance
of performance. Stadler's clarinet concerto, too, I
began, oh, maybe two years ago. I can't waste time
finishing things that won't pay.

Then some pieces I want to keep for myself,
like my variations on Figaro's aria, Benucci's "*Non
più andrai, farfallone amoroso*," "No more games

with the girls, little Cherubino, little Cupid." I've played those variations often, but maybe I'll never write them down! If I sell them, no one will ask me to play them again. Now I play them and people toss me a ducat, or some trinket—a watch, perhaps. Typical of these people—they don't realize that what we need is cash ... We were given all those snuffboxes when we were young Papa said we should open a shop.

Do you think, if you leave all these fragments behind, that someone else may finish them?

Why? Haven't they ideas of their own? Of course, we all use each other's ideas—but only themes, not half-finished pieces.

Whose ideas have you stolen?

Stolen! *Used*, not stolen. A few themes, a few combinations. I've used ideas by the London Bach, and Handel—and Clementi, that sonata theme was just right for the *Magic Flute* overture. I had to hurry to write that after returning from Prague. Clementi didn't see the possibilities. I made it into a little fugue—just as much fugue as the public can take …

Some might call that plagiarism …

Of course it's not. It's using a model—we all do it. Sometimes it's a whole piece—you imitate it as a way to learn. Long ago I did this with Haydn's quartets … I was very young then, so his are better! I also learned the opposite way. I wrote an aria for Aloysia, as different as possible from the setting I loved, by Bach. Maybe you know the poem, *"Non sò d'onde viene quel tenero affetto,"* "I don't know where this tender feeling comes from"? It was a love token, too …

Yes, some people steal. I heard in Paris that there was some trouble involving Gluck. I forget if he used someone's aria, or someone robbed *him*. But with arias it's easy to forget. Singers carry them in their luggage—fit them into an opera to suit their voices. But it's better to write a new one that fits voice and opera, as I've done for Aloysia and that nice Luisa Villeneuve who sang Dorabella in my *School for Lovers*.

I hate to think what happens when I'm not around. I hear *Don Giovanni* in Frankfurt and Mannheim is in *German*! No recitatives. I'd hardly recognize it!

Would you want put that right, claim ownership?

You can't. They'd laugh at me. And I suppose the music's still mine. So if they like it, perhaps one day those theaters will ask me for a new opera—and pay!

THE SALZBURG YEARS

Mozart spent much of his life in Salzburg, a
small independent city-state heavily dependent
on the Habsburg monarchy, although not
formally part of Austria—in fact, Mozart and his
father called themselves German musicians.
The Prince-Archbishop of Salzburg maintained
a substantial *Kapelle*, a body of musicians whose
function was to adorn the cathedral liturgy and
entertain the ruler, his entourage, and guests.
The musicians contributed to the city's cultural
life, and music played a part in domestic
entertainment. Mozart's retrospective
perception that he couldn't work in Salzburg
is not borne out by his high productivity during
his time there.

May we go back to the beginning? Your birthplace. How did a provincial city like Salzburg suit a brilliant young musician like you?

Ah, you know of Mozart the *Wunderkind*. How tiresome that became. In Paris when I was 22 they still thought I was seven years old, a beginner … But I'm a grown man! I have a wife and children. What's to become of them if I don't get over this fever …? I'm sorry, I'm confused. What did you ask about?

Salzburg, where you started your life and career.

It was home. Mamma was there—she didn't always travel with us—and my sister was there, Nannerl. And Papa, and the dog. But as a child I traveled to Vienna, Paris, London, and then to Italy. Salzburg was proud of me the first time we came home, three years abroad and Nannerl and I had grown into little adults—she must have been, what, 15? I suppose I was 10. Later, I wasn't so special. In the end I couldn't stand the place. There was plenty of music, but not all good—and not enough opera! Too much for the Church!

But wasn't the Church your employer?

Yes, but it didn't pay much. And it's the same words over and over again in the services—work becomes routine. And the musicians were sloppy—poor ensemble, wrong notes. They'd turn out for duty's sake, then slip away for a drink. Sometimes the drink came first … We had more fun with winter concerts and university serenades in summer. There I could try new ideas, and the musicians were interested, they'd play better. Happy days! There was time for outdoor games, too. We liked shooting at targets dressed up to look like people we disliked. It helped us carry on when things were hard, or work was dull.

Who did you work for in Salzburg, apart from the Church?

Oh, the great and the good. The nobility. The Haffner family. I remember writing a big serenade for one of their weddings. Years later Papa made me write them a symphony. I was in Vienna and busy, yet I broke my back to finish it in time. Small thanks I got … Yes, the rich. They could play, some of them. Like Countess Lodron, I wrote a concerto for her and her two daughters—for three claviers! One of them could hardly play at all. One has to please such people.

Were Salzburg's musicians really so bad?

Ah well, to be fair, not all of them. There was Papa!

Always sober, always hard-working. He should have been *Kapellmeister*. And Haydn—not Papa Joseph, but his brother Michael—he's still at Salzburg, and isn't likely to leave. He likes his drink, but he's a fine composer. I admire his church music a lot, and his symphonies. I performed one in Vienna—with improvements ...

Old Schachtner—one of the court trumpeters and a violinist, too—he frightened me with his trumpet when I was small. And he tricked Papa—he had me play the violin alongside him, then stopped playing and I carried on. Before that Papa thought I couldn't play. Schachtner wrote poetry for my unfinished opera ... *The Seraglio*—not the Vienna opera, but another one like it, *Zaide and Gomatz* we might have called it.

But those were German musicians. The Italians— well enough trained, but no better than Papa—were always better paid! Brunetti, the first violin, played my music well enough, but I didn't trust him. He would sneak to the Archbishop to curry favor. Ceccarelli the castrato was all right. Of course, he didn't have a wife (don't laugh). So we were family for him. Then other interesting people came by—that French pianist, Madame Jenamy. I wrote my best concerto for her—best so far, anyway. She played it well. But later I played it better!

Was Madame Jenamy a better player than your sister?

No, no. Nannerl is a wonderful player. I've known many women musicians—my students, little Cannabich, Ployer, Auernhammer—but Nannerl was best. I'm sad she couldn't do more. She composed well—songs and so on—but gave up. I'm afraid Papa was only interested in me … Now she has too many stepchildren. Miserable life, living miles out of town.

We lost touch. I know she didn't like Constanze. So it is with families. So it is with life! It all looks rosy as a child, but things break apart ...

But back to you. Why did you decide to leave Salzburg?

I was suffocating! I couldn't work. In other cities— Munich and Mannheim and Vienna—I could breathe.

So who suffocated you?

His Highness and Mightiness, the Archbishop. Colloredo. Colicoredo! Old Schrattenbach, who came before, was all right—he let us travel. Papa said he even gave us money. And so we made Salzburg famous all over Europe.

What was your quarrel with Colloredo?

He liked music—even played the violin—but he didn't like too much of it. A little in church, or at his table. He didn't care for Salzburg or its reputation. Nothing mattered but his own glory and his status in Vienna. Musicians were only servants … But I'm better known than him through my talent and hard work. He was just born rich. Nobody likes him. He called me lazy however hard I worked. But I am *not* a servant! And I won't lick his backside.

So you left his service?

I *wanted* to leave. But you can't resign. It's not done to leave the service of a prince. He knew I wanted to go and he wouldn't let me. Pure spite. I had to make him fire me. Vienna was right for me—I would *not* go back to Salzburg. So I insulted him. In the end his chamberlain, Arco, booted me out, and that was that.

Did you consider revenge?

Ha! Of course. It's not charitable, I know. He was
only doing his master's bidding … But I wanted to
pay Arco in his own coin—a nice, swift kick where it
would do most good. I'd probably have been arrested.
Whipped! It did happen if you affronted these
arrogant bastards. And they've friends and relations
everywhere, it wouldn't do to get in their bad books.
I'd be blackballed and starve. So I stayed in Vienna,
made friends there, and never went back to Salzburg.

Really? Never?

Now you remind me, I did once. With Constanze.
But by then I was doing well in Vienna. The Emperor
liked me, so the Arch-Booby couldn't touch me.

GETTING AWAY FROM HOME

Mozart was a city dweller and any popular music he had contact with was urban. Besides the capital cities of Europe—London, Paris, Vienna, Prague, and Berlin—he was attracted to smaller German courts, where princes lavished money on music. The most notable of these in Mozart's life was the Elector of Mannheim, Carl Theodor, who kept perhaps the finest orchestra in Europe. He moved to the larger center of Munich in 1779, and commissioned Mozart's most lavishly orchestrated opera, *Idomeneo* (1781). Mozart probably wanted to try his luck again in London; Paris he had tried, without success, in 1778. Under Joseph II he had been happy in Vienna, but there was a new Emperor now and times were changing.

You've lived in Vienna for ten years now. Have you ever thought of leaving? And if so, where would you go? Somewhere you know from your early travels perhaps?

Like Paris? That brings back unhappy memories. My dear mother … so sad. If only she'd agreed to see a French doctor. It had to be a German and we wasted time finding him, just a quack. She wasn't bled soon enough … No, I've had enough of Paris.

I can understand that. Where else might you have gone?

Perhaps London. The good king and queen love music, do they not? I hear King George has been ill—mad, some say … Better now? Good, good. My old friends like the London Bach and Manzuoli—the great castrato!—are dead, or gone away. But I have other friends there—Nancy Storace, my first Susanna in *Figaro*, and her brother Stephen—you know him, a good composer! I've had invitations for the opera—but that impresario, O'Reilly, am I right, he's not reliable, probably a charlatan? The violinist Salomon is a true musician. He's made plans for concerts, but wanted Papa Haydn first. If that works out, perhaps I can follow Haydn to London! But it would be difficult, with the family …

Yes, I have good memories of London, even when Papa was ill. We were only children and had to keep quiet, so I sat down and wrote a symphony! Nannerl nudged me to make sure I didn't forget the horns—their parts can be so boring. But people kept testing us, as if we were some kind of monkey—silly tricks like playing without seeing the keys and improvising arias. I wrote a vocal piece for their new museum [the British Museum]—in English! "God is our refuge and strength." Very bad, I suppose. I hope they've lost it!

I believe they still have it ... How about Italy? Could you have lived there?

Italy! That first visit was wonderful—Florence, Rome, Naples, Venice, and Milan of course. My first grand serious opera in Italian. Ah, the *opera seria*—the noblest type of opera. It bored the Emperor, so we've not had much of that kind in Vienna lately. Young Archduke Ferdinand, in Milan, he liked my music, but nothing came of it. Papa tried to persuade the Grand Duke of Tuscany to take me on. We waited ages for a reply—it was no—and now he's Emperor, so he's got me anyway! But then I was too young to be a *Kapellmeister*. And there are so many Italian *maestri*. Too many. They look after their own. They don't want Germans. But so many Italians go abroad! Piccinni in Paris, Paisiello in Russia, Salieri here in Vienna. No, for Italy I'm a German pianist. Not Wanted.

And how about Germany?

I'd loved to have stayed in Mannheim. Perhaps if I'd got a job there, I would have married Aloysia instead of her little sister …

Would that have been a good thing?

No. But at that time I never looked at little Stanzerl. It was Aloysia's voice I loved. The Elector of Mannheim liked me, and his wife—I dedicated pieces to her. Or Munich maybe. I composed my great opera there, *Idomeneo*. I put in everything I knew and it was well performed—the Elector liked it! But still no job.

Were there any other cities you found promising?

Berlin I liked, two years ago. We never went as

children. The old King was a dangerous fellow.
Always at war. And my father—a loyal Catholic—
couldn't live with Protestants! I don't mind them!
When I got home I started quartets for the King and
sonatas for the Princess, but I never finished them,
and I sold the quartets I finished for next to nothing,
to pay the rent.

Where else have you traveled as an adult?

Frankfurt, last year, for the coronation of our new
Emperor. Not much fun—my fault, for preparing
such a long concert. People had to leave early and
that never looks good … But Prague's another thing!
It's my kingdom, they love my operas there, and the
orchestra's good. But it's just an opera company—no
court and not enough rich people! Nothing I could
live on. And so back I come, to Vienna …

VIENNA, CITY OF THE CLAVIER

Center of a sprawling and cosmopolitan empire
ruled by the Habsburgs, Vienna was not a large
city by modern standards, but in the 1780s it
could boast outstanding cultural diversity. At
this time, the relatively new pianoforte took over
from the harpsichord in popularity, and Mozart
was its finest exponent. Within eighteen months
of Mozart's arrival in the city, his opera *The
Seraglio* was performed and admired. But while
Mozart remained central to Vienna's musical
life, he had continually to reinvent himself to
make money. And his teaching income was
unreliable, since the wealthy left the city for
their country estates each summer, depriving
Mozart of work.

What attracted you here to Vienna?

It's the city of the clavier! Vienna really is wonderful. Or was … Everything's changed now, though. The Emperor leaves to make war, then he dies. Half the nobility leave, too … or make economies. Perhaps they don't want my kind of music any more. Fashions change. Those concerts—when I couldn't find subscribers—what a humiliation! Symphonies and concertos ready, but no public.

In the early years I was all the rage. So many Viennese friends—all kinds of people: musicians, theater people, singers, and poets, like Stephanie, my poet for *The Seraglio* and that silly play *The Impresario*. Da Ponte's a good fellow, too—for an Italian … I miss him.

These are professional colleagues and friends. What kind

*of relationship do you have with your audience—the
nobility? And your friends outside the world of music?*

So many friends … Now I'm feeling ill I wish I could
call on my dear doctor, Barisani. We knew his family
in Salzburg. He was younger than me, but he died.
Death! The goal of our existence, the truest friend
of mankind—that's a bit of philosophy for you. I said
that to my father and I try to believe it. But it's hard.

I see. Coffee? Or perhaps another beer?

Hot punch, please. What were you asking me about?

The Viennese nobility?

Ah yes. Count Hatzfeld, a dear friend and fine
violinist. He died just before Papa … I wrote a nice

solo for him—the violin obbligato for *Idomeneo* in that private theater, the Auersperg one—when his sister-in-law sang. I was so moved, hearing my grandest opera again at last—the only time it was staged in Vienna.

Some of these people could have earned a living in music, but they're lucky, they didn't have to. Gottfried—Baron von Jacquin—and his sister were good friends. I composed that trio with viola and clarinet for her to play with me and Stadler. I wrote it while they were playing skittles. And little things for Jacquin—songs, nocturnes—so he could pass them off as his own.

You didn't mind that?

What are friends for? Then there were my brothers … So many!

Freemasons, you mean?

Yes! Hofdemel, Puchberg—true friends and brothers.
They lend me money. Never as much as I ask for, so
I ask for more than I really need! I pay them back as
soon as I can. In the Lodge we're equal, all brothers.
That matters so much after what happened with
the Arch Donkey. I believe Freemasonry began
in England—is that so? I'm a regular Englishman,
you know! Strange that so many fine people are
Freemasons—Born (a great scientist and great mind),
noblemen, even clerics. Why does the Church
distrust us? The Emperor—Joseph—he always
wanted to control everything, even the theater, even
funerals! Can you believe we must be buried in a
sack, so we rot away as quickly as possible! Joseph,
yes, he was always interfering—he reorganized the
Lodges. You'd think we were plotting a rebellion or

something. Ridiculous! The Esterházy family—not the prince Papa Haydn used to work for, but his relations—could they be called rebels? My funeral music was used when one of them died. I composed other things for the Lodge, too. Serious pieces … though the words aren't great poetry. I wasn't working for the Church, which was a refreshing change, and it was good to work in a serious style.

There's Count Lichnowsky, too. I traveled in his coach to Prussia. Then he had to get back, and borrowed 100 gulden from me. From me! Compared to him I have nothing! But he loves music. Without such men we would all starve. Of course, I borrowed from him, too—oh God, that lawsuit. He sued me for the debt. I have to pay it back, but surely he'll allow me time … But I mustn't burden you with my troubles.

ENTERTAINING EMPERORS

From 1765 Emperor Joseph II ruled the
Habsburg Empire with his widowed mother,
Empress Maria Theresia. After her death,
he ruled alone until dying, aged only 49,
in 1790. From 1781 Joseph was Mozart's
principal patron, admiring his keyboard
playing, but less convinced of his ability in
opera. Nevertheless, he encouraged the court
theater to perform *Figaro* and *Così fan tutte*.
The cultural achievements of Joseph's reign are
remarkable, but liberal reforms were rescinded
before his death and in 1788 he embarked
on an unsuccessful Turkish war. Joseph was
succeeded by his brother, Leopold II, for
whose coronation as King of Bohemia Mozart
composed *La clemenza di Tito*.

What were your relations with the Emperor Joseph?

He supported me. He was good to me. Even when
I was a child. I don't think it was his fault that my
opera buffa—*La finta semplice*—didn't get staged.
My father blamed the Emperor, then he blamed
the court composer—Gluck himself!—and then he
blamed the Italians. That was more likely! But Joseph
died too soon. He made me *Kammermusikus* on 800
gulden a year—too little for what I could have done
and too much for what I did, for I did nothing! But
only because he didn't ask—he was at war, then he
was ill. Luckily the new Emperor has kept me on. But
he doesn't want chamber music, he's lived too long
in Italy. He just wants a few dances for the New Year
balls, and I can write them in my sleep.

Doesn't dance music interest you musically?

Not much. Though I have fun with rhythms or an unusual orchestra—like the one with sleigh-bells, my father liked that sort of thing—and when I use tunes they all know, like "*Non più andrai*" from *Figaro*.

When you settled in Vienna, what did you do for Joseph?

It's what Joseph did for me! I couldn't have survived without his interest. He loved good clavier playing, and I could play anything at sight—sometimes improving it as I went along. He understood what I was doing. But for a long time the Emperor didn't understand that I can write operas, too. My success in Italy as a boy was all forgotten. It wasn't easy to prove myself. Joseph did allow me to write a German opera—you know, my *Seraglio*. It was a success, so what did he do? He closed down the German opera and replaced it with an Italian company!

That must have been a disaster?

It was upsetting for the singers. There's German opera at the *Kärntnertor* and some went there, others joined the Emperor's new Italian opera. But the Italians didn't like it—and did I mention that they were always paid more? Some came to Vienna for a season or two, then disappeared. Some brilliant, some mediocre, but always changing.

But didn't you write for the Italian company eventually?

Again, thanks to Joseph! The Italians didn't like the fact that I was German. No one found me a good libretto. Not for years. I chose *Figaro* myself. It's had plenty of performances, but back then—five years ago—we were taking a risk. It's long, it's difficult. And Joseph had banned the play it's based on. Politics!

ON POLITICS AND REBELLION

We learn very little from Mozart himself
about his political sympathies. His library was
dispersed, so we don't know what he read, and
in his last years, with his father dead, Mozart's
letters are almost devoid of content that isn't
professional or personal. In spite of his
dependence on the rich and powerful, Mozart
seems to have held liberal views on social
mobility and an enlightened notion of human
value, independent of rank. These opinions,
and his professional frustration, contributed
to his rebellion against Salzburg's ruling
Prince-Archbishop.

Why did you say you're a regular Englishman?

In England people feel free. Isn't that so? That's what matters, not systems. And it's not just about meeting King George in the park—you could do that here, with our Emperor … at least, with Joseph. The English king and queen heard Nannerl and me play, and, what's more, they paid us at once! Here, outside the walls of the Lodge, I have to be polite to people who aren't worth a kreutzer, but were born high and mighty. Because they pay the bills. That's true in England, too, but there the people in the middle of society respect artists. We're not servants! My father thought of settling in England, but he couldn't bear the religion. I wouldn't mind it, though there'd be no scope for my kind of church music.

So you don't set much store by political theory?

Of course, I do think about politics. But for me it's about whether I can work as I wish to. I could do that in Vienna, or in other places, like Berlin.

What do you think of the French Revolution?

What revolution? I heard that a crowd freed prisoners from the Bastille, but there were only a few of them. It was about the time *Figaro* was revived in Vienna—two years ago, when it had many more performances. What's a revolution? You English killed your king long ago, but there was soon another one back on the throne—and there's still a king in France. Surely the French won't make that mistake? I met her, of course, the French queen, when I was a child—Archduchess Maria Antonia—I promised to marry her when I grew up! I didn't know that would never be allowed. I was, what? Six? That did no harm, though she didn't help me later in Paris. The French king has no ear for music. There was this possibility of going to Versailles as organist, but it would have been like being buried alive. I prefer the theater. And in Vienna I can have both theater and church.

Is it fair to say your attitudes to politics and other nations are based on music and patronage?

Certainly. I don't want revolution. I'm paid by the nobility, the Church, and a few people who'll buy their titles in due course. I get support from Jews, too—mostly those who've become Catholics, like Da Ponte. You know Goldhahn, a brother Mason—he's lent me money. Then Baron Wetzlar was godchild to my poor little Raimund, my eldest … Emperor Joseph liked such people. Jews, Gentiles—it didn't matter as long as they worked for what he wanted.

Of course, we cut the political bits out of *Figaro*—when Figaro says the Count got where he is "By taking the trouble to be born." That's in the play, I liked that. But we couldn't say it out loud. No point in writing an opera that can't be staged.

So there was political freedom in Vienna under Emperor Joseph?

Maybe more than now. Yes, that Salieri opera, *Axur*, is about overthrowing a tyrant. It went down well in spite of the music …

That thought seems to make you smile, Herr Mozart …

Yes, yes—sheer mediocrity, I'm afraid. But the public liked it, all the same! Our dear Viennese …

VARIETY AND NOVELTY: MOZART'S INSTRUMENTAL MUSIC

Mozart's output of magnificent sonatas, chamber music, serenades, concertos, and symphonies was large only by the standards of a later era. After he escaped the feudal world of Salzburg to become an independent artist in Vienna, Mozart found concert-giving to be one of his most lucrative activities, fueled by the incessant production of new works. The series of concertos began with pieces Mozart considered easy to enjoy, but with ideas only connoisseurs would fully appreciate. As Mozart's rapport with his orchestral players developed, he composed far more elaborate woodwind parts, also increasing the length of movements and varying the conventional forms.

Why have you written so much instrumental music?

Have I? Look at other composers. Papa Haydn's written many more symphonies, quartets, sonatas. Not to mention Boccherini and Vanhal. Too many pieces, too much alike! I like writing instrumental music, it's always been part of me. But I write what I can sell. Piano quartets didn't sell, so I wrote trios.

Could you tell me about your concerts? How do you put together a program?

A symphony to begin, but with the finale at the end. In the middle, my concerto—best if it's new, or new to the city I'm in. Then a couple of arias, depending on who'll sing for me if I play for them in their benefit concerts. An improvisation. Variety. The public wants familiar things, yet also novelty, so you write new pieces, but not too different from previous ones.

What do you think makes a good concert?

The music should have novelty, but not be too new
in style—mix the new with what's expected. I tricked
them in Paris by starting my finale quietly—to cries
of "Sshh!"—then wham! In came the whole orchestra,
and they loved it. Cries of "Bravo!" They got what they
wanted, the great *tutti*, but differently—delayed.

During the music?

Sure, why not? So it was a success. But I couldn't
really enjoy it, my mother was dying …

I'm sorry … perhaps we could move on to another topic?
I've been told that audiences find your music difficult.

Sometimes, I confess, I've tried too hard to interest them. I don't like people to sit there chattering. I want them to attend, to be surprised—but in a way that pleases them. Look at my clavier concertos. I try new ideas—different forms, a larger orchestra, bringing in the piano with a new tune instead of the one the orchestra's just played. That sort of thing—and finer harmony. In my Concerto in F, a fugue—a fugue's fine if it's not too long, otherwise they'll think it's "learned" and "scientific" and so on. Such nonsense … A bit of fugue's fun, and fits with my other ideas. Perhaps the Concerto in C Minor was tough for the Viennese—and *Don Giovanni*. They're more willing to listen to new things in Prague. But why not in Vienna? Surely they will … I hope I'm here to see it …

Indeed! What about your father, did he understand your difficult music?

He was from an earlier generation, but he kept up. He told Nannerl there were mistakes in my clavier Concerto in C. I supervised the copying myself—there were no mistakes. But those long, slow dissonances— so beautiful—perhaps badly played by those Salzburg hacks so they sounded wrong. I don't know, I wasn't there. It sounded well in Vienna! But Papa liked the Concerto in D Minor that I wrote the same year. Of course, he heard *me* play it, I had that big clavier with pedal-board. Papa had that young cub Marchand play it in Salzburg. A good pianist, that boy, and a fiddler, but willful. Yes, my father—he kept up better than most. Storm and struggle he could handle—the opening of my Concerto in D Minor, syncopated, "dum daá daá daá," then "brrm" in the bass. But the C Major? Strange that Papa couldn't understand my slow movement ... It haunts me now—so beautiful, like a lament in an opera ... then consolation ...

OPERA PEOPLE

Between 1782 and 1790, Mozart wrote *The Seraglio*, *Figaro*, *Don Giovanni*, and *Così fan tutte*. At first, their wealth of ideas, ingenious ensembles, long finales, and sumptuous orchestral sonorities marked them as difficult. Da Ponte tells us that Emperor Joseph called *Don Giovanni* "tough meat for the Viennese." "Let them chew it," retorted Mozart. In the long run, he was right. The tuneful but relatively simple operas of his contemporaries were forgotten until our historically conscious age. The public digested Mozart and, ever since, has been nourished by his wit, pathos, sharp characterization, and exquisite timing.

I understand the public here likes your beautiful operas less than they deserve. How do you feel about this? What's your approach to writing opera?

It's a job, like any other!

But do you see your operas only as musical works? Or do they instruct us about life, love, politics? Even morality?

I don't think of them that way—those meanings are in the words. Though the words belong with my music, of course. I don't do what Gluck did—take bits of one opera and put them in another, with different words!

So the words matter more than the music?

No! A thousand times no! The poetry must serve the music. Poets shouldn't have too many ideas of their own. The public wants arias, duets, quintets—nowadays even in *opera seria* like *Tito* and in German operas just as in *opera buffa*. Finales, too! My *Magic Flute* finales are as long as those in *Figaro*. And more complicated, with changes of scene. So the music must take charge or it's a muddle!

Of course, the poet *thinks* he's in charge—he lays out the plot and directs the actors—but I know when something won't work. With *Idomeneo* I wrote endlessly to Papa from Munich and he spoke to the librettist in Salzburg—that clerical prig Varesco. I had to promise all his verbiage would be printed. It would never work on stage. I had to cut, cut, cut! You see, they weren't all good actors. My old friend Raaff—he was already 66!—was stiff as a board as Idomeneo, though at least he sang tolerably. But that boy—*mio molto amato castrato* Dal Prato—I had to teach him every note, like a child. And even I could act better ...

What counts is theater. Words and music are a means to an end. I've known the theater from childhood. I saw operas in Vienna and Italy before writing any. When I was a boy, I couldn't do much about the poetry. Luckily it wasn't all bad! But with *Idomeneo*, my grandest *opera seria*, I knew more about theater than Varesco—or Papa, who tried to tell me what was what. *"Basta!"* as Papa used to say—enough! He meant well, but I had my way.

What of your librettist, Lorenzo Da Ponte?

That phoenix—a true poet for the theater! It's strange, he'd written nothing before coming here and the Emperor made him court poet!

He wrote librettos for other composers. Did that worry you?

No, why should it? He needed the money. He wrote
for Martini, Salieri, Righini, Storace—a good one,
Shakespeare's *Comedy of Errors*. Now I think of it,
that would be a good name for most *opera buffa*!
Here in Vienna, his *Cosa rara* with Martini put my
Figaro in the shade—but not in Prague! Martini's easy
to listen to. I was more ambitious. I can't regret that.
He or Salieri could never have written *Don Giovanni*.

Or Così fan tutte?

The *School for Lovers*? Not the way I did it. That
libretto was meant for Salieri, you know, but he
decided he didn't want it, or thought he had too
much work. Though he doesn't write half as much
as I do! When the libretto came my way, Da Ponte
changed a lot, because I insisted. Salieri might not
have bothered!

How were the singers in Prague?

Good enough in *Figaro* and *Don Giovanni*—but not
as smart as the Viennese. In *Tito* they were old-
fashioned, but all right. I wanted tenors for the hero
and his friend, but *Tito* was an *opera seria*, so we had
to have a castrato … and the friend was played by a
girl in trousers! The Emperor—and Empress—were
in Florence for years and have Italian taste. Castrati!
I've known some good ones. That cantata for
Rauzzini—what was it? *Exsultate, jubilate*. Now he's in
England—perhaps you know him? Yes, a good enough
fellow. So is Bedini—my Sesto in *Tito*—a bit fat, but
a good singer. And he worked well with my clarinet
solo for Stadler, in the aria "*Parto, parto*"—starting
grandly, getting faster, each section more brilliant.
Even though he says "I'm going, I'm going," he stays
there singing! In *opera buffa* that would be funny.

MORALITY AND MEANING:
MOZART'S OPERAS

Two centuries after their composition,
Mozart's operas generate philosophical debate,
literary interpretations, and sequels. *The
Seraglio* reflects rivalry between Christian and
Islamic empires, *Don Giovanni* has an implicit
Catholic framework. *Figaro* invites political
interpretation partly inspired by its source,
Beaumarchais's *Le mariage de Figaro*. *The Magic
Flute* may reflect Masonic ideals, but is also
in the fairy-tale tradition exemplified by *The
Philosopher's Stone*, to which Mozart contributed
in 1790—magical plot, good versus evil, serious
and comic characters, spectacular scenery,
and (especially in *The Magic Flute*) every type
of music, from the folk-like to the learned.

Why did you compose Figaro?

Well, it's funny, and touching. It's also realistic—human—not like most opera. Papa thought the play tiresome. It's long, but a good play. Of course, it was banned. It offended the French king and his queen, Marie Antoinette—the Emperor's sister. Wretched politics! Set to music, politics would just be dull—page after page of dry recitative. I can write that while working out something else—or while asleep—but my fingers ache because there's no reason to stop and think! No, we left out the politics, and so we have Figaro all jealous because he thinks Susanna will betray him with the Count. He's unhappy—obsessed—and the music goes round and round. That's where I take over from the poet! Just saying the words hasn't half the effect. In an aria, I can repeat them over and over—he's bewitched by the woman, but now she's a bear, a dove, a rose covered in thorns. Round and round it goes in his head, *"il resto nol dico, già ognuno lo sà ... il resto nol dico, già ognuno lo sà,"* till he feels dizzy. And then come the horns—"tarantá, tarantá, tarantá"—*cuckold's* horns, of course: "the rest I needn't say, all men know that."

Yes, thank you! Who needs Benucci when you can hear the composer himself! But back to why you wrote Figaro.

I was simply desperate to write an *opera buffa*. I wanted to compose for those group singers: Benucci, Storace, Mandini. I read a hundred librettos—none any good. I made a couple of false starts. Then came Paisiello's *Barber of Seville*—they got it from St. Petersburg. *Figaro* is the play that comes after it in Beaumarchais's series, so that was the obvious thing to do—it's got the same characters! The singers picked their roles—Storace decided on Susanna, as she's in nearly every scene. Benucci was the star and Figaro's the best role. I could see the other *buffo*, Bussani, was unhappy—he sang Figaro in *The Barber* and was stage manager, too! We were in mortal dread that he'd sabotage the whole thing … But that's how it is in theater. The poet and composer have to serve these touchy people—who are paid much more—or they head back to Italy. But it's worth it. Nothing's better than a fine opera.

But isn't Figaro seditious? The Count wants to exercise his right to sleep with Susanna, though he's abolished the droit de seigneur …

So? He's a count and a swine—what's new? *Opera buffa* is full of such people. Even *Cosa rara*. Ah, that aria, *"Vedrò, mentr'io sospiro, felice un servo*

mio?"—"Must I suffer while my servant is happy?"
Hypocrite! He's angry, but there's nothing to be
angry about. All Figaro's doing is getting married!
But I put the Count's anger into the music—seething
violins, down the scale, two octaves, then that
shuddering trill … He's dangerous, one could
write like that in *opera seria*. But in the end the
Count's fooled and says sorry, so humbly, in front
of everyone! Aristocrats *can* be fair. He could
have Figaro arrested, but doesn't. And Figaro's as
impertinent as ever I was to the Arch-Booby!

I see! So your operas are *moral?*

Why yes, some very much so. The Pasha in *Seraglio*
is filled with desire for revenge, threatening torture,
but then he forgives his enemy's son. In the end
it's just his stupid servant, Osmin, who's furious,

wanting revenge, and I made him comical by using Turkish music—cymbals, drum, and triangle. Don Giovanni ends up in hell. What do they all sing? *"Questo è il fin di chi fà mal, E de' perfidi la morte alla vita è sempre ugual"*—"That's how the wicked end, their life and death are just the same." A little fugue to round things off … It was good to hear the final scene again in Prague, in Vienna we had to cut it …

Then there's Tito: the opera's about him being merciful. It's written into the title: *"La clemenza di Tito"*! And *The Magic Flute* is funny, with Schikaneder's antics—Papageno! Typical of Schikaneder, dressing himself up as a bird and making all those jokes because he's terrified—he thinks the lions will get him, or the dreaded Queen (my dear sister-in-law). But it's serious, too. That ass Goldhahn has a good heart and lends me money, but he kept laughing at the serious bits. I couldn't bear it, I called him "Papageno" and made myself scarce. I hope he's not offended, but I don't think he even understood the insult! Offence, fun, morals— it's up to the audience. Talk to two people afterwards and they might have been at a different show.

And your School for Lovers? *Isn't that frivolous?*

School for Lovers! Now, that *is* a bit of fun. But serious, too. Everyone's betrayed except Alfonso. Tears are shed, but they make up at the end and are the wiser for it. Is that not moral? Anyway the characters aren't real people! Who could believe those disguises? Albanians? Ridiculous! Yet I felt sorry for Fiordiligi, trying to be true to her lover—even though I can see it's just the singer Ferrarese on stage running up her scales or booming away on her low notes. There are disguises in *Don Giovanni*, too. And *Figaro*. But in those it's night-time—you can believe people would be fooled. They change clothing—Giovanni and Leporello, the Countess and Susanna—and Benucci and Storace mimic Giovanni and the Countess.

You've mentioned changes made for different productions—arias cut and so on. Did that improve Don Giovanni?

Alas, no. The new arias for Vienna are good. But Prague saw the real *Don Giovanni*. It was their idea, the impresario gave Da Ponte that feeble Venetian libretto and we worked it over—fewer characters, doing more, more ensembles and finales, and a lot of fun …

Emperor Joseph thought your music was not good for singers.

Ask *them*! Ask old Raaff. Or Madame Wendling—in *Idomeneo* she was so happy, *arcicontentissima*. Ask Storace—my Susanna!—or Benucci, or Aloysia. No, the idea that my music isn't good for singers really annoys me—I write well for them all. Yet others manage the same arias! Aloysia did all right with Donna Anna. Duschek sings the big aria from *Figaro* that I made for Ferrarese. And so on …

Do you believe opera seria *has a future?*

Perhaps. Things change, we have this new Emperor. I'd like to write more *opera seria*. But first we must do *Tito* again—and finish it properly! I never wrote the simple recitatives—no time. We all thought Salieri would write the Coronation opera, but it was left to me. He thought he was too busy, as usual …

Writing *The Magic Flute* in Schikaneder's

summerhouse was much more fun. All for good friends and a good company. Anna Gottlieb—in *Figaro* she was a little girl, but now she's all grown up and a regular princess—she's Pamina. And my sister-in-law Josepha, Frau Hofer, she's Queen of Night. Can't act, but those high notes! Like stars … Her husband, the violinist, is a good friend. Schack is Tamino and Gerl, Sarastro. They like working with me …

But you weren't asking about this. Yes, I'd like to write more *opera seria*—even if it means using more poems by old Metastasio … For *Tito* I wrote in my catalogue, "Opera by Metastasio turned into a real opera by Mazzolà."

Was that not unkind?

To Metastasio? He's dead, and fashions change. His stories are too complicated for modern music, and he always has three acts. Two's better. It's fine to tell the story in simple recitative, then let everyone take an aria in turn and walk off like peacocks, but I want my characters to react to each other. Mazzolà's version of *Tito* dealt with that—there are ensembles and a real finale. It's not just for the action, it's for contrast—*chiaroscuro*. And that goes for the characters, too. Best is to have some serious, some comic, and some *mezzo carattere*, in-between, mixing opposites. Unfortunately, that's not allowed in *opera seria*! Comedy makes the serious more effective, and vice versa. So perhaps in the end I prefer *opera buffa*.

Do you prefer Italian or German words?

Yes.

Excuse me?

Both. But I'm German and now in Germany—even in Vienna—more than ever is sung in German. So it's "Don Juan" for "Don Giovanni" and in Prague the "School for Lovers" is *Eine Machts wie die Andere*." I'd rather have it written in German in the first place! Songs are good in German: *Lieder*! We have good poets. I set Goethe's *The Violet*. That's something *new* we Germans can do. If only professional singers would notice how effective songs can be, then we'd compose more, and sell them, too! Maybe in the future ... And as for German opera? A sequel to *The Magic Flute*. If only I could ...

I've seen it once—I go again tomorrow. I couldn't understand everything, so can you tell me what it's all about?

Life. Everything. Marriage—happiness—goodness

and wickedness … if you think it's complicated, you should have seen *The Philosopher's Stone* last year. I told Schikaneder if he wanted an opera composed entirely by me, it must have a clearer outline, despite all the little episodes, comedy, and so forth. *The Magic Flute* is like a lot of our German operas—comic and serious together. How I love that! And a quest— the search for good. At first the Queen seems good, but she's ambitious, scheming for power. She's even prepared to sacrifice her own daughter.

Is it about the opposition of men and women? And perhaps about the Freemasons?

There's something for everyone. You mustn't think I—or Schikaneder—agree with what those priests say about women—"Be on the watch for women's wiles"—as if they're all the same, *cosi fan tutte*, as it were … absurd! But that's part of the test, the trials the prince goes through to understand whatever it is he understands at the end … One doesn't spell out such things in opera. The music takes over. Schikaneder used to be a Freemason himself, so he worked some of those ideas into the words. But we don't reveal any secrets! It could be any old religion—Egyptian, or something … or any old philosophy. That first finale, when the old priest comes out from the temple of wisdom, that's some of the noblest music I've written. And the characters aren't Freemasons. True, the priests are all men, but there are women in the temple. It makes a proper chorus. Better than church where you have to write for boys—they won't let women sing, and you can't always get castrati, they're a dying breed … I suppose you can't call them a breed! But I like working with the choir at St. Stephen's here in Vienna.

SACRED MUSIC, BELIEF, AND FILIAL DUTY

Mozart composed most of his sacred music early in his life and it is relatively neglected. Understanding of his religious beliefs is confused by the mistaken notion that Viennese Freemasons were subverting organized religion. There is no more reason to associate Mozart with Enlightenment tendencies to atheism than with political revolution. If Mozart did not receive communion before he died, it was only because his condition worsened suddenly. According to Mozart's sister-in-law, a priest visited him and administered extreme unction reluctantly because the patient hadn't asked for it himself, but no conclusion should be drawn from the behavior of one churlish priest.

May I ask about your religious beliefs?

I'm a good Catholic. Quite good, anyway ... I'm no saint! I don't think about my Savior every hour of the day. If Papa was right, and my gift comes from God, then it's my duty and destiny to compose. But I can honestly say I believe in one God, *"Credo in unum Deum."* I attend Mass. What else should I do?

Isn't Freemasonry opposed to the Church?

But how? The Emperor himself isn't a better Catholic than most of my brothers in the Lodge. And I've met clerics who were—shall we say—not perfectly moral. Da Ponte! He's an Abbé, but has love affairs. Surely he's as good a Christian as the Arch-Donkey—a petty tyrant. If they were all like *him*, I couldn't respect the priesthood.

Do you read the philosophers?

I don't read much—no time! Papa read a lot and talked with these people when I was a child. I remember writing him from Paris that Voltaire had died—I said the godless fellow had perished as he deserved, like a dog. I'm sorry I said that. Voltaire was a great writer. But I thought it would please Papa. Then my mother died and we forgot all about it, but now I think it wouldn't have pleased Papa. And it wasn't charitable.

Did your father control you too much when you were young?

How much is too much? I don't know. Control me he did, like I control my little Carl! But as I grew up I tired of it. When I left home to seek my fortune, Papa wrote all those letters, so long and packed with names—possible patrons, people who might introduce me to other patrons—the Duke of this, Madame de that, Abbé the other. Perhaps we'd met some of them when I was a child. But it was useless, years later, to recall such favors! It made me seem forward, above my station, as the grand people saw it. Papa blamed me for my reticence. He had this thing about your countrymen: "With nobility you can be quite natural, but with other people, be more like the English"—meaning don't be frank and open! Well, I'm not being English when I talk to you! But he would go on, as if he hadn't brought me up properly: "My dear Wolfgang—take your medicine—say your prayers." And those letters when I was in Mannheim: "I read your letter with shock and alarm—you always embrace the first wild scheme that comes into your head—*off with you to Paris*." Paris! The worst mistake of my life …

Did the "wild scheme" involve Aloysia?

Indeed it did! I said I'd take Aloysia to Italy and make
our fortune. Well, Papa was right there—she's a good
singer, but not the best ...

*You've mentioned your mother's death often, how did
your father react to that?*

It's strange. He's heartbroken, but all solicitude—
worried about me. He sends me black powders, for
goodness' sake, as if Mama's death would give me
a fever, or make me constipated. Then he's bitter.
I'm accused of not coming home fast enough. But
I had to see if there was a chance of a decent job
somewhere! But no, Papa persuades the Archbishop
to make me court organist, so we're all together
again in Salzburg—a tight little family, me struggling

with the organ and choir and orchestra. When I was fired for staying in Vienna, that was worse! Then I'm lazy, improvident, willful, easily led astray—and promiscuous! That I never was! I was spied on. That Peter Winter—not a bad composer, but a bastard—sent lies about me back to Salzburg. How could they believe him? Those letters were cruel—they hurt so much I had to burn them. Papa said his life was wasted. He'd sacrificed his career for me … and I didn't love him. We patched things up, but it was never the same. He couldn't accept that I was grown up, wanted a wife, wanted my own place. I was to provide for his old age. I did send him money … when I could. Not much. And I sent him my music—having it copied wasn't cheap, I can tell you. May God rest his soul.

Amen. And now you're composing a requiem! But it's unfinished as yet …

Yes, yes, and my distinguished patron is no doubt getting impatient … But I've had so much to do—two operas, Stadler's clarinet concerto, and the cantata for the Masons, none of them could wait. And I haven't written church music since I left Salzburg. Getting started wasn't easy …

But you composed a Mass – in C minor—a few years ago.

How could I forget? It's gigantic. Or it would have been – it isn't finished. I wrote it to thank God for my marriage and the birth of my first child, my little Raimund … Perhaps he would have become a *real Kapellmeister*. I don't think Carl will be a musician—he's too interested in other things and, besides, he's a bit lazy. Yes, the C-minor Mass. We performed bits in Salzburg and Constanze sang—better than I expected! But I couldn't finish it … I still thank God for my marriage, but when we got back to Vienna, Raimund was dead. The saddest thing … Perhaps we should have reared him differently, some mothers feed their children at the breast. But if Constanze had done that, we couldn't have gone away without him. Those nurses—you have to watch them all the time. Yes, the Mass. I arranged it for the society of musicians—an Italian cantata on the penitence of King David. There was no place for such a Mass in church in Vienna—far too long. And the solo Constanze sang in Salzburg isn't for choirboys!

In my last years in Salzburg I wrote two grand Masses and each year a set of vespers—"Gloria Patri" after every psalm—and the litanies. "Kyrie eleison," "Lord have mercy," so often. It taxes one's invention, setting the same words over and over.

So why did you choose to work at St. Stephen's?

The obvious reason! Money, security. And I like my invention to be taxed. But I've written nothing for Vienna till now. And church music is part of me— part of my musical being, out of use for years. So I'm happy to do a requiem, and I wrote that little thing for Baden, "Ave verum corpus." I'd like to do more in that style—simple, affecting, reverent, yet so modern. I like the ancient style—yes, even the fugues!—but this feels new, something I can make more of. Though, of course, it's like the music for the priests in *The Magic Flute* ...

But that opera is about ancient Egypt, or Freemasonry, not Catholicism ...

How can music know the difference?

Now it's my turn to say "touché!"

REQUIEM

Late in 1791, Mozart drafted a petition to the Habsburg heir, Archduke Franz, promoting his ability in church music with a view to further employment. The Requiem was commissioned anonymously, though Mozart may have known that his patron was Count Walsegg, whose wife had recently died. The Count fancied himself as a composer, but deceived no one when performing music by others under his own name as, eventually, he did Mozart's Requiem, which was completed after Mozart's death by Franz Xaver Süssmayr.

Mozart, I see you're not feeling well, but please excuse me if I press you once more. I remember you saying, "Requiem—easy!" How can that be?

I meant easy money. Writing it's not so easy. But 25 ducats in advance! Half the fee before I start! That helped with bills when Constanze was taking the cure. And 50 ducats is half what I get for an opera, but nothing like half as much work. It's shorter. No choice with the words—no arguments with a poet! The orchestra's easier, too. The same all the way through, that's the tradition. Trombones help the chorus or it goes out of tune. Trumpets and drums for the glory of God—but then the fires of hell need them, too! And timpani. Not much wind—no horns!— just bassoons and basset-horns. Soft, somber—right for a funeral.

I don't say it's easy to write good church music.

I don't think much of Salieri's, by the way. Haydn's, I admire ... But it was decent of Salieri to use some of my pieces for the Coronation. No, writing the piece is hard work—and not just the fugues. But I learned with old Martini and had plenty of practice in Salzburg. And I studied old Bach's music at Swieten's, and Handel. All these years in Vienna I've wasted those skills ... and the Requiem's not finished ... I hope Count whatever-his-name-is doesn't want his money back.

This is your first requiem. Do you have a model?

A fine one from Salzburg—Haydn—ages ago from the old Archbishop's funeral. I played in the orchestra, I was about 15, and I've never forgotten it. Handel's been going around in my head since Swieten got me to adapt "Messiah" and other pieces. There was

more I might have done for him: oratorios, "Judas,"
"Joseph." Too simple for today, Handel's orchestra—
mostly just strings. But such ideas, such dignity!

There's a funeral anthem that—to be frank—I
used to get me going. It was for an English queen—
Caroline, I think. Yes. It's the Introit that begins the
Requiem. And that fugue, "Kyrie eleison"—again!
Can one ask for mercy too often?—the old subject
with the falling seventh. We all use that from time to
time, but now I've used Handel's second subject as
well, the semiquavers: "Christe eleison." I did more
with it than him! I chopped off the first few notes for
contrast—the words fit either way—and most of his
piece isn't a fugue at all—it turns into great cries of
"Hallelujah!" And he's in D major, the key my father
liked because it makes the violins sound brilliant,
even with trumpets—like my Haffner symphony—the
one Papa persuaded me to write in such a hurry.

Where was I? Yes, the Requiem. Well, in the "Kyrie" I changed Handel's ideas into D minor.

Tricks of the trade! Perhaps I shouldn't be giving them away—I take it you're a student! But why not? If you're any good you'll need them. Fugues are still hard work for me. I don't always sketch things out, but fugues, yes. It's the first part that's hard. Once you get the lines in place against each other, the *ars combinatoria*, it's not so bad. I've sketched the Amen to end the Sequence, but I haven't composed the Sequence yet—I moved on to the Offertory. Putting off the evil hour … Of course, the Sequence fugue is on the same theme I use all through—that plainsong, "Tonus Peregrinus". It's in the Introit. It'll be everywhere … if only I get my strength back to finish it.

Herr Mozart? I'm sorry to be keeping you so long. You

look tired. Would you like some coffee? Perhaps more

punch, some food? I'd be honored ...

I know what you're thinking. Don't say it. You've
caught me in time. I really am ill. Shall I recover ...?
This time I feel weaker than ever. Well, if I die now,
maybe Constanze can salvage something from the
Requiem—and get the rest of the fee. She'll need it.
I've written the best half. Maybe Eybler could do
something, he understands good church music. Or
Haydn. Or old Abbé Stadler. Better not be that ass
Süssmayr ...

I'm haunted by those words in the Offertory,
"de morte transire ad vitam"—"through death we pass
into life." Ah, yes. This is the music I've just been
writing ... the weaving violins, and that harmony ...
Eternal light ...

NOTES

LANGUAGE

With titles of Mozart's works, I have been guided by common practice. Titles that are names, such as *Don Giovanni*, remain in the original language. *Le nozze di Figaro* is usually called *Figaro* (as it was by Mozart). The laconic nature of some Italian titles means we have no elegant translation, and they remain in their original language: for example, *Così fan tutte*, not 'Thus Do All Women." This opera is also referred to as *The School for Lovers* (*La scuola degli amanti*), the title apparently preferred by its librettist, Da Ponte. German titles are given in English: *The Seraglio* for *Die Entführung aus dem Serail*, *The Magic Flute* for *Die Zauberflöte*.

INSTRUMENTS

In his early years, Mozart learned the harpsichord, but later mainly played the fortepiano (an early version of the piano). Much of his earlier music sounds well on either. Both are covered here by the generic term Mozart used, *clavier*, rather than its English equivalent, "keyboard," which today has other (digital) connotations.

CURRENCY

The gulden (florin) was the unit of currency most used by the Mozarts. It is reckoned (Spaethling, 2000) that 20 gulden had the purchasing power of approximately US$600 or £350 at the time of writing. The other unit of currency employed in Austria was the ducat, worth 4½ gulden. Thus, Mozart's fee for an opera could be expressed as 100 ducats or 450 gulden. The gulden was divided into 60 kreutzer (each kreutzer, therefore, was worth approximately 50 US cents).

REFILL?

BIBLIOGRAPHY

Emily Anderson (trans. and ed.), *The Letters of Mozart and his Family*, third edition in one volume (Basingstoke: Macmillan, 1985)

David Cairns, *Mozart and His Operas* (London: Penguin, 2006)

Peter Clive, *Mozart and his Circle* (New Haven: Yale University Press, 1993)

Otto Erich Deutsch, *Mozart: A Documentary Biography* trans. Eric Blom, Peter Branscombe, and Jeremy Noble (London: A. & C. Black, 1965)

Cliff Eisen, *New Mozart Documents* (London: Macmillan, 1991). A Supplement to O.E. Deutsch's *Documentary Biography*

Cliff Eisen and Simon Keefe (eds.), *The Cambridge Mozart Encyclopedia* (Cambridge: Cambridge University Press, 2006)

Jane Glover, *Mozart's Women: His Family, His Friends, His Music* (London: Pan Macmillan, 2005)

Robert W. Gutman, *Mozart: A Cultural Biography* (New York and London: Pimlico, 2001)

Simon Keefe (ed.), *The Cambridge Companion to Mozart* (Cambridge: Cambridge University Press, 2002)

Albi Rosenthal and Alan Tyson (eds.), *Mozart's Thematic Catalogue* (London: The British Library, 1991). Contains a facsimile of the manuscript list kept by Mozart from February 1784.

Julian Rushton, *Mozart: An Extraordinary Life* (London: Associated Board of the Royal Schools of Music, 2005)

Julian Rushton, *Mozart* (New York: Oxford University Press, 2006)

David Schroeder, *Mozart in Revolt* (New Haven: Yale University Press, 1999)

Robert Spaethling, *Mozart's Letters, Mozart's Life* (New York: Norton, London: Faber & Faber, 2000)

William Stafford, *Mozart's Death* (London: Macmillan, 1991; pub. in the USA as *The Mozart Myths*, Stanford University Press, 1993)

INDEX